PARTY HATS

FOLD ON DOTTED LINES AND PASTE
TRIANGULAR FOLDS SECURELY
BEHIND FRONT OF HAT
AS SHOWN BELOW.
HOOK TAB IN SLOT
AND PASTE.

CUT

TAB

SLOT

FOLD
AND PASTE

FOLD
AND PASTE

PASTE

CUT IN TO
DOTTED LINE

SLIT A

FOLD

CUT IN TO
DOTTED LINE

FOLD TAB ON
DOTTED LINE

FOLD UP

SLIT B

TAB A

FOLD UP

FOLD
BACK

FOLD
BACK

TAB B

NUT CUPS
WITH ATTACHED PLACE CARDS

CUT OUT CAREFULLY AND FOLD AS DIRECTED.
INSERT TAB B IN SLIT B IN BACK OF CUP.
(SEE FIG. 1.)
FOLD UP BOTTOM AND PASTE SIDES
ON INSIDE OF CUP. SLIP TAB A
THROUGH SLIT A AND PASTE.
(SEE FIG. 2.)

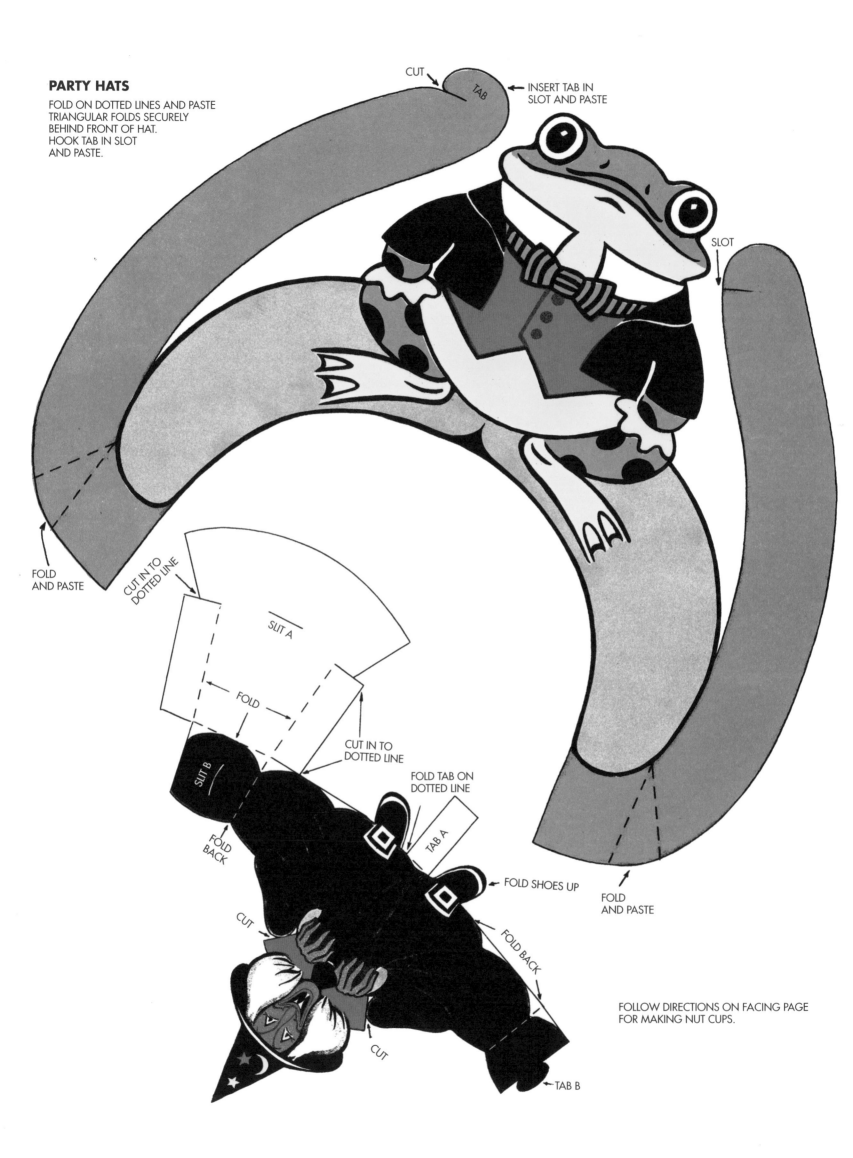

PARTY HATS

FOLD ON DOTTED LINES AND PASTE
TRIANGULAR FOLDS SECURELY
BEHIND FRONT OF HAT.
HOOK TAB IN SLOT
AND PASTE.

CUT

TAB

INSERT TAB IN
SLOT AND PASTE

SLOT

FOLD
AND PASTE

CUT IN TO
DOTTED LINE

SLIT A

FOLD

CUT IN TO
DOTTED LINE

SLIT B

FOLD
BACK

FOLD TAB ON
DOTTED LINE

TAB A

FOLD SHOES UP

FOLD
AND PASTE

CUT

FOLD BACK

CUT

TAB B

FOLLOW DIRECTIONS ON FACING PAGE
FOR MAKING NUT CUPS.

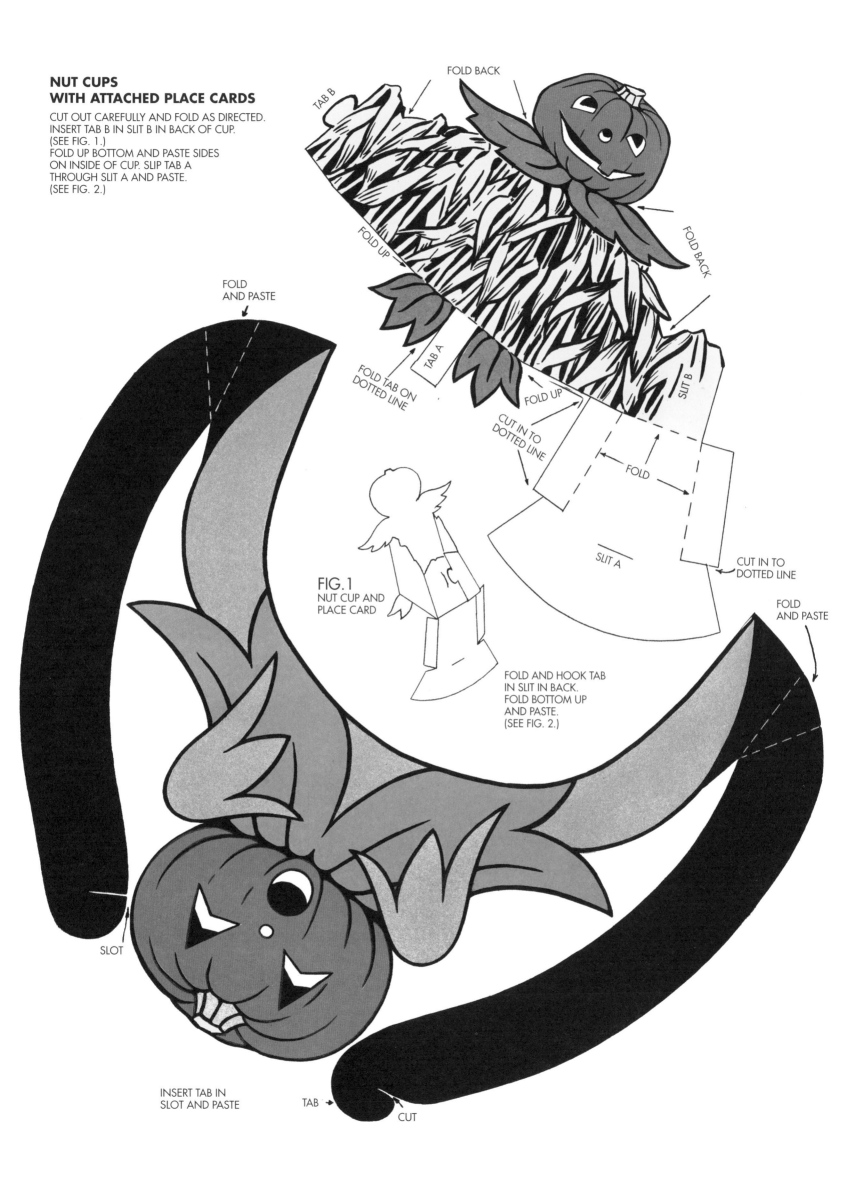

NUT CUPS
WITH ATTACHED PLACE CARDS

CUT OUT CAREFULLY AND FOLD AS DIRECTED.
INSERT TAB B IN SLIT B IN BACK OF CUP.
(SEE FIG. 1.)
FOLD UP BOTTOM AND PASTE SIDES
ON INSIDE OF CUP. SLIP TAB A
THROUGH SLIT A AND PASTE.
(SEE FIG. 2.)

FOLD BACK

TAB B

FOLD UP

FOLD BACK

FOLD
AND PASTE

TAB A

FOLD TAB ON
DOTTED LINE

FOLD UP

CUT IN TO
DOTTED LINE

FOLD

SLIT B

FIG. 1
NUT CUP AND
PLACE CARD

SLIT A

CUT IN TO
DOTTED LINE

FOLD
AND PASTE

FOLD AND HOOK TAB
IN SLIT IN BACK.
FOLD BOTTOM UP
AND PASTE.
(SEE FIG. 2.)

SLOT

INSERT TAB IN
SLOT AND PASTE

TAB

CUT

TOP FOR PUMPKIN

SLIP OVER TOP OF PUMPKIN AS SHOWN ON
FRONT COVER.

CUT

CUT

CUT
OUT

CUT

FOLD BACK
ON DOTTED LINE

CUT

NUT CUPS
WITH ATTACHED PLACE CARDS

SEE DIRECTIONS ON OTHER PAGES.

TAB B

FOLD BACK

FOLD BACK

FOLD UP

FOLD TAB ON
DOTTED LINE

TAB A

FOLD UP

FOLD UP

SLIT B

CUT IN TO
DOTTED LINE

FOLD

SLIT A

CUT IN TO
DOTTED LINE

WITCH

CUT OUT AND FOLD SKIRTS
BACK. HOOK TABS MARKED X
TOGETHER ON INSIDE. FOLD
HEAD ON DOTTED LINES AND
SLIP HAT BRIM OVER HEAD.

FOLD
HEAD
BACK
ON
DOTTED
LINES

CUT TO
DOTTED LINES
ON BOTH SIDES

FOLD
BACK

FOLD
FORWARD

FOLD
BACK

CUT ALONG
TOP OF SKIRT

FOLD
BACK

INSERT IN SLOT A

CUT

X

SLOT A
CUT TO DOTTED
LINE

CUT
OUT

FOLD
BACK

FOLD BACK
ON DOTTED LINE

BRIM FOR HAT

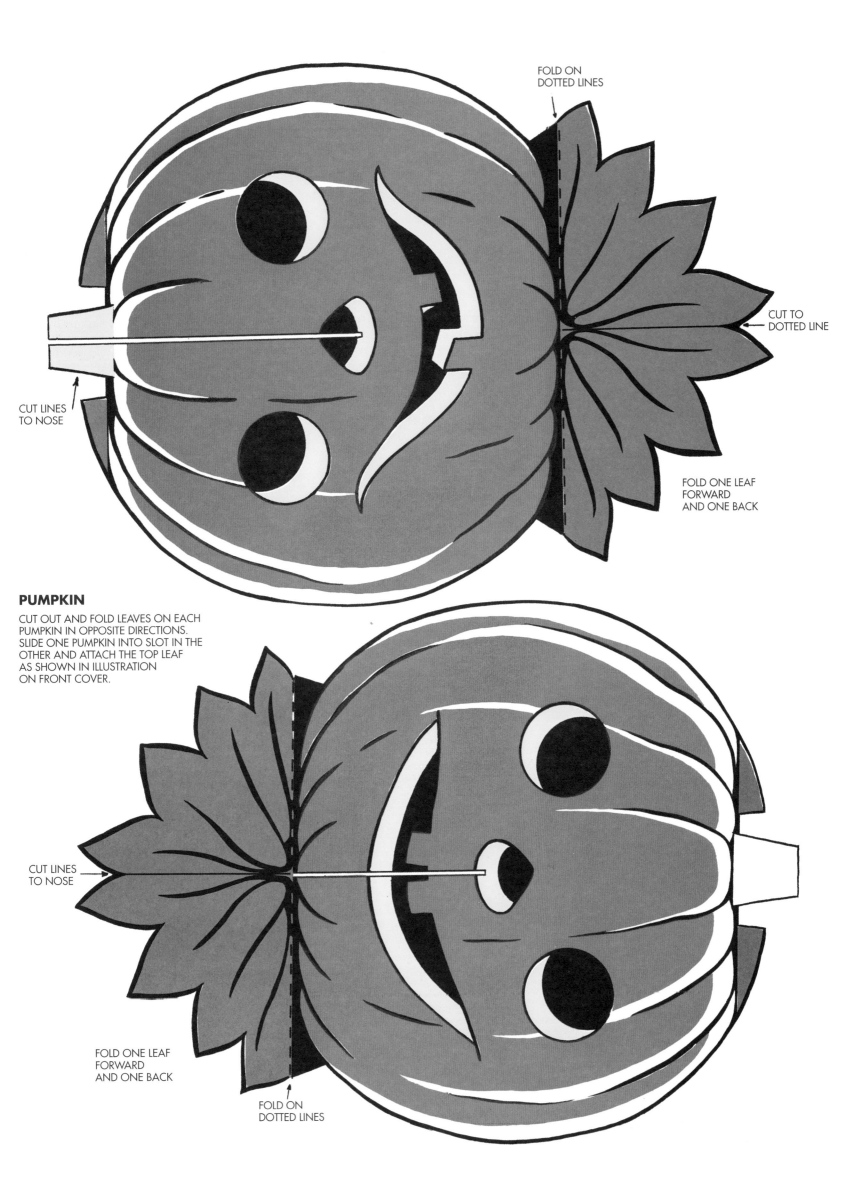

FOLD ON
DOTTED LINES

CUT TO
DOTTED LINE

CUT LINES
TO NOSE

FOLD ONE LEAF
FORWARD
AND ONE BACK

PUMPKIN

CUT OUT AND FOLD LEAVES ON EACH
PUMPKIN IN OPPOSITE DIRECTIONS.
SLIDE ONE PUMPKIN INTO SLOT IN THE
OTHER AND ATTACH THE TOP LEAF
AS SHOWN IN ILLUSTRATION
ON FRONT COVER.

CUT LINES
TO NOSE

FOLD ONE LEAF
FORWARD
AND ONE BACK

FOLD ON
DOTTED LINES

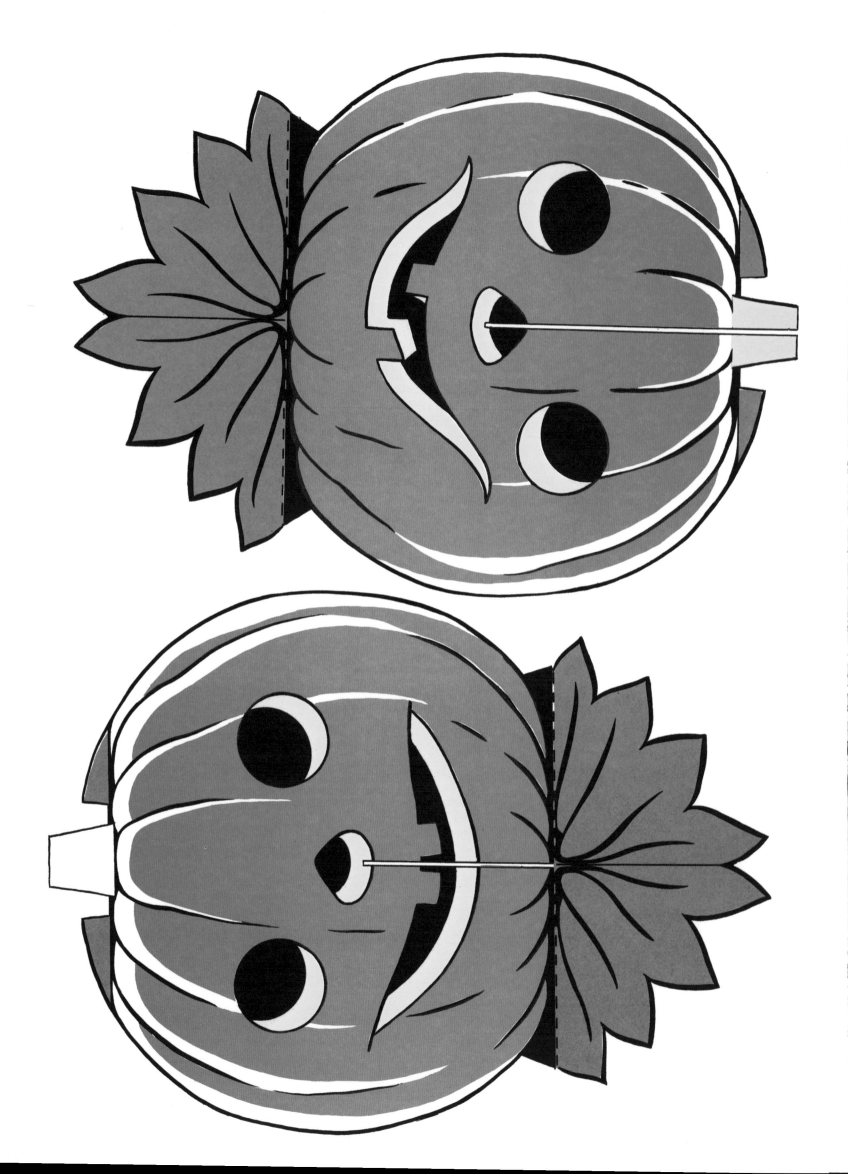

PARTY HATS

WORN AS IN ILLUSTRATION
(SEE OPPOSITE PAGE FOR
DIRECTIONS.)

INSERT TAB IN
SLOT AND PASTE

CUT

TAB

SLOT

FOLD
AND PASTE

FOLD
AND PASTE

CUT IN TO DOTTED LINE

SLIT A

FOLD

CUT IN TO
DOTTED LINE

FOLD TAB ON
DOTTED LINE

FOLD UP

TAB A

SLIT B

FOLD UP

FOLD BACK

TAB B

FOLD BACK

**NUT CUPS
WITH ATTACHED PLACE CARDS**

FOLLOW DIRECTIONS ON OPPOSITE PAGE
FOR MAKING NUT CUPS.

NUT CUPS
WITH ATTACHED PLACE CARDS

CUT OUT CAREFULLY AND FOLD AS DIRECTED.
INSERT TAB B IN SLIT B IN BACK OF CUP.
(SEE FIG. 1.)
FOLD UP BOTTOM AND PASTE SIDES
ON INSIDE OF CUP. SLIP TAB A
THROUGH SLIT A AND PASTE.
(SEE FIG. 2.)

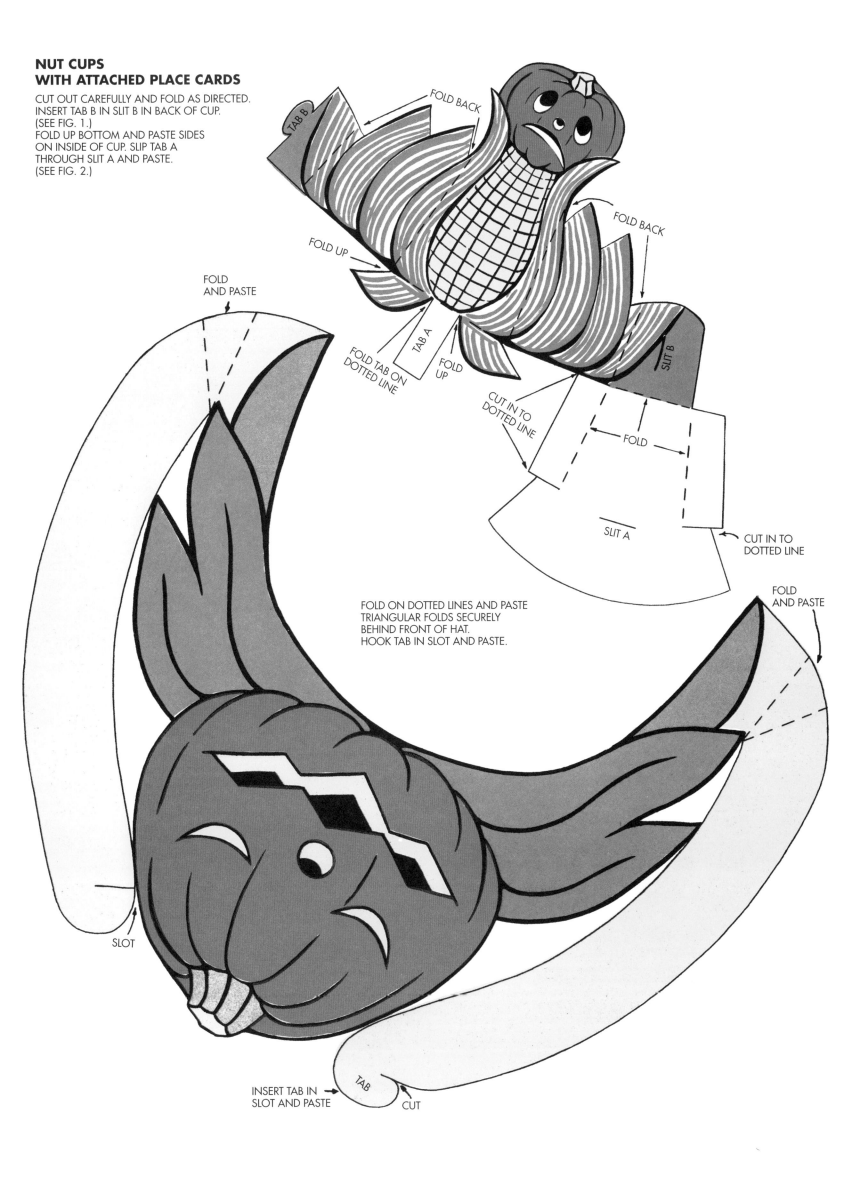

TAB B

FOLD BACK

FOLD BACK

FOLD UP

FOLD
AND PASTE

FOLD UP

FOLD TAB ON
DOTTED LINE

TAB A

FOLD
UP

SLIT B

CUT IN TO
DOTTED LINE

FOLD

SLIT A

CUT IN TO
DOTTED LINE

FOLD ON DOTTED LINES AND PASTE
TRIANGULAR FOLDS SECURELY
BEHIND FRONT OF HAT.
HOOK TAB IN SLOT AND PASTE.

FOLD
AND PASTE

SLOT

INSERT TAB IN
SLOT AND PASTE

TAB

CUT

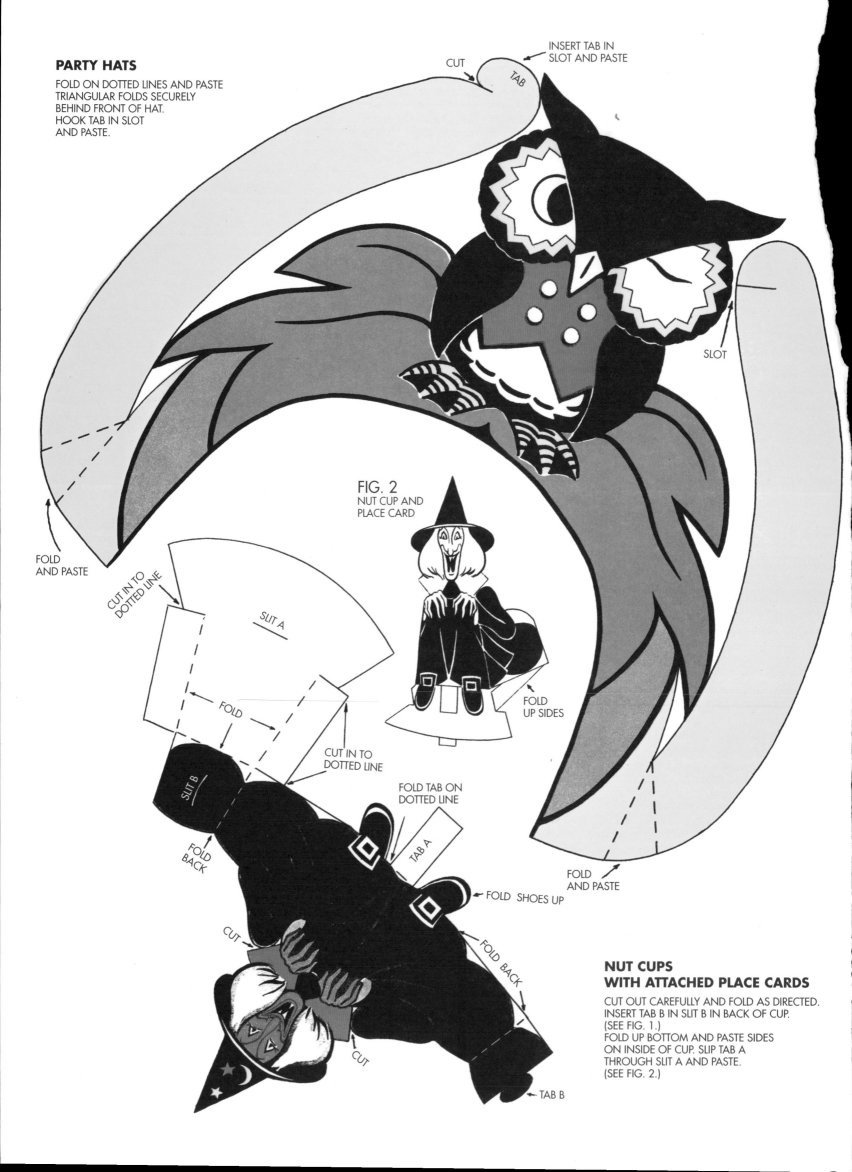

PARTY HATS

FOLD ON DOTTED LINES AND PASTE
TRIANGULAR FOLDS SECURELY
BEHIND FRONT OF HAT.
HOOK TAB IN SLOT
AND PASTE.

INSERT TAB IN
SLOT AND PASTE

CUT

TAB

SLOT

FOLD
AND PASTE

FOLD
AND PASTE

FIG. 2
NUT CUP AND
PLACE CARD

CUT IN TO
DOTTED LINE

SLIT A

FOLD

CUT IN TO
DOTTED LINE

SLIT B

FOLD
BACK

FOLD UP SIDES

FOLD TAB ON
DOTTED LINE

TAB A

FOLD SHOES UP

FOLD BACK

CUT

CUT

TAB B

**NUT CUPS
WITH ATTACHED PLACE CARDS**

CUT OUT CAREFULLY AND FOLD AS DIRECTED.
INSERT TAB B IN SLIT B IN BACK OF CUP.
(SEE FIG. 1.)
FOLD UP BOTTOM AND PASTE SIDES
ON INSIDE OF CUP. SLIP TAB A
THROUGH SLIT A AND PASTE.
(SEE FIG. 2.)